Disney
MONSTERS AT WORK

MEET THE MONSTERS!

From the Employee Files of Monsters, Inc.

Random House New York

 Published in the United States by Random House Children's Books, a division of Penguin Random House LLC, 1745 Broadway, New York, NY 10019, and in Canada by Penguin Random House Canada Limited, Toronto, in conjunction with Disney Enterprises, Inc. Random House and the colophon are registered trademarks of Penguin Random House LLC.

rhcbooks.com

ISBN 978-0-7364-4256-5 (trade)

Printed in the United States of America

10 9 8 7 6 5 4 3 2 1

MONSTERS, INC

A message from the desk of James P. Sullivan

To: All Monsters, Inc., Employees

It is with great appreciation for all the support I've received from my fellow employees here at Monsters, Inc., that I accept the role of CEO of this fine organization.

In this position, I hope to usher in a new and prosperous direction for our company. We will, from this day forward, transition from powering our beautiful city with Scare Energy to powering it with Laugh Energy.

I know this is a dramatic change for our dedicated team of scary monsters. But I believe in the power of laughter—TEN TIMES more powerful than screams – and I know that we will all work our hardest to make sure Monsters, Inc., remains the greatest power company Monstropolis has ever seen!

So what are we waiting for, monsters? Let's get those giggles!

Yours truly,

Sulley

Waternoose being taken away by the CDA agents.

MEMO

INTRODUCING OPERATION
LAUGH IT UP

Operation Laugh It Up will be a major relaunch for Monsters, Inc., incorporating new energy-capture initiatives that will increase our dominance in the field.

PHASE ONE

- Introduce Operation Laugh It Up to employees
- Humans Aren't Toxic, and Neither Are You lecture series

PHASE TWO

- Rewire Simulation and Control Rooms with Gigglewatts gauges
- Identify former Scarers for enrollment in Mike's Comedy Classes
- Rebranding: replacement for We Scare Because We Care

PHASE THREE

- Beta test of Laugh Floor
- Tally test laugh totals
- Set quotas and finalize Launch Team members
- Find our funny!
- Cross all fingers, tentacles, and extra appendages and hope for the best

REBRAND NOTE: Send to Monstropolis Energy Regulatory Commission for approval:

IT'S LAUGHTER WE'RE AFTER

MEMO

BACKGROUND ON THE TRANSITION TO LAUGH POWER

Under the leadership of Henry J Waternoose, former CEO and mentor of Randall Boggs, Monstropolis's premier energy company, Monsters, Inc., barely skirted bankruptcy. Waternoose, along with his partner in crime, Randall, embarked on a plan to kidnap a thousand human children and extract their screams.

Their devious plot was thwarted by James P. Sullivan, who revealed Waternoose's confession to the Child Detection Agency (CDA). With the company in even more jeopardy, Sullivan became the new CEO. Fortunately, in those troubled times, his colleague and best friend, Mike Wazowski, discovered the power of laughter and realized that a better business model would be to harness Laugh Power instead of screams.

The current challenge, and it is not a small one, is to rebuild and retrain the Monsters, Inc., staff so we can establish the new mission with a high level of success.

MONSTERS, INC., EMPLOYEE POLL

1. How comfortable do you feel scaring kids?

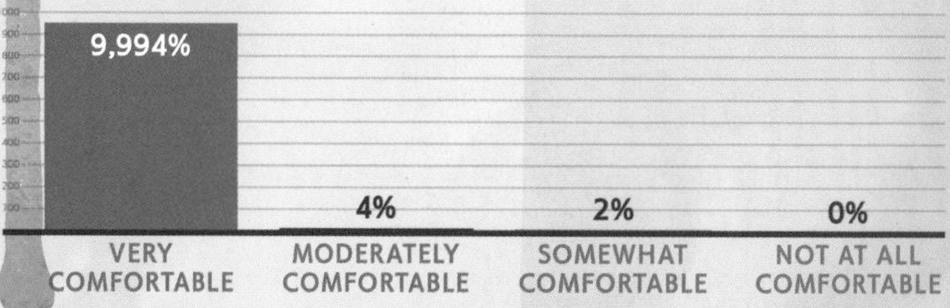

2. How comfortable do you feel making kids laugh?

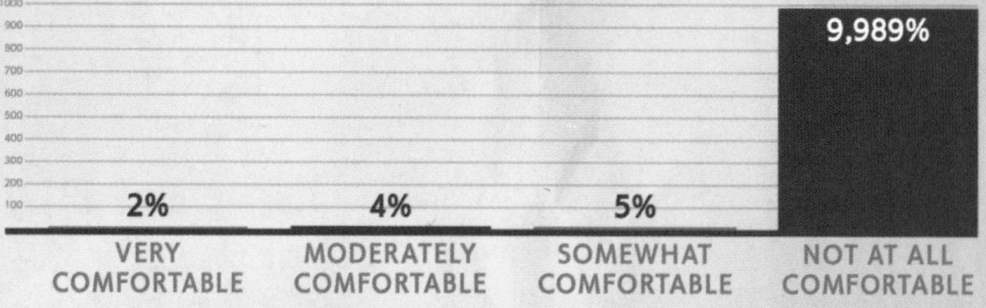

3. On a scale of 1 to 1,000, with 1 being "would rather drink a gallon of Chalooby slime" and 1,000 being "already practicing my spit takes," how eager are you to participate in our retraining program?

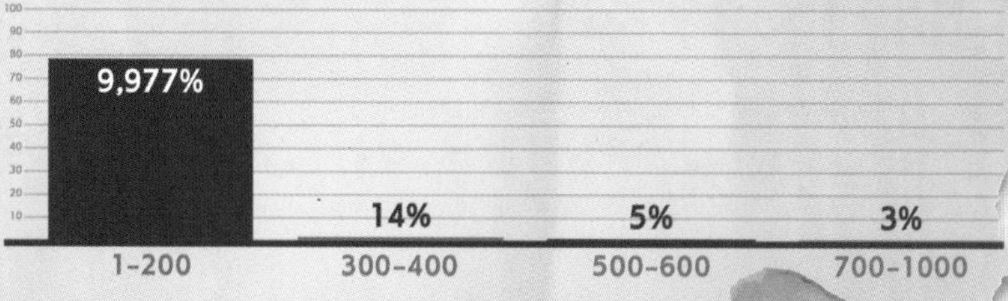

INTERNAL: NOT FOR CONSUMPTION

MONSTERS INC

BRINGING YOU THE POWER OF LAUGHTER

THE MONSTERS, INC., FUN ~~FACILITIES~~ TEAM

AKA MIFT

The members of the Monsters, Inc., Facilities team are the monsters behind the monsters—the ones who keep the factory running, grease the gears, and wrench the nuts!

Although MIFT toils behind the scenes, their work is critical. They're responsible for handling all the repairs at Monsters, Inc., from keeping the door vault operating smoothly to keeping the toilet from clogging after Pauly has been in there.

TYLOR TUSKMON

STRENGTHS: 2x Ultimate Frisbee champion, award-winning rancid chili sludge chef

WEAKNESSES: Clumsiness, lack of real-world experience, always has fresh breath

PERSONAL HIGHLIGHT: Making the entire fourth grade scream at the Shockington Elementary scare play

GOALS: Following in the footsteps of his idol, James P. Sullivan, and becoming Top Scarer

FAVORITE CLASSES: Origins of Fear, Canister Design, Toxicity Studies, Roars and Whispers, Intro to Doorknobs, Silent Tactics II

EMERGENCY CONTACT: Bernard and Millie Tuskmon, father and mother

*KEEP FAR WAY FROM BREAKABLES—has already knocked over a cart of laugh canisters with his horns.

Note to self:
Replace broken office lamps

TYLOR TUSKMON

Monsters Inc.
Office of Monster Resources
RE: Acceptance Status

Tylor Tuskmon
Applicant No. 1211919520518

Dear Mr. Tuskmon,

Monsters, Inc., is pleased to offer you the position of Scarer! Your superior scaring skills and commitment to your studies at the School of Scaring make you an ideal fit for our company.

Please arrive Monday morning at 9:00 am and report to Ms. Flint to receive your scare assignment.

Sincerely,

Henry J. Waternoose III

Henry J. Waternoose III
CEO, Monsters, Inc.

Tylor Tuskmon

EDUCATION

- 44.0 GPA
- Monsters University School of Scaring
    - Graduated Scarum Cum Laude
    - Class Valedictorian

EXPERIENCE

- Tuskmon Hardware
    - General Assistant to owners (parents), after school, on weekends, and when grounded

TYLOR TUSKMON

MEMO

REASSIGNMENT OPTIONS:

- Hat rack
- Umbrella hanger
- MIFT

REASSIGNED

Family owns hardware store — reassigned to MIFT

FIRST DAY ON THE JOB

- 8:40 a.m. – Arrived 20 minutes early
- 9:00 a.m. – First day officially begins!
- 9:20 a.m. – No longer hiring Scarers?! WHAT!
- 9:21 a.m. – Existential crisis
- 9:22–9:27 a.m. –
- 9:30 – Called mom. Went to voicemail.
- 9:30 a.m. – Sent to New Employee Orientation for reassignment

Tylor sets new scaring records at Monsters University School of Scaring.

The job offer from Monsters, Inc., arrives right after graduation.

Tylor arrives bright and early Monday morning.

Tylor eagerly waiting.

Tylor reports to Ms. Flint for his scare assignment.

Tylor learns that there's been a change at Monsters, Inc.

Tylor gets reassigned to MIFT.

Val, Tylor's old classmate and new coworker, takes Tylor to the MIFT offices.

Tylor gets warmly welcomed to MIFT, despite the fact that Fritz didn't have time to make a new sign.

Tylor gets his official Monsters, Inc., hat and ID and embarks on his new dream of becoming a Jokester.

VAL LITTLE

STRENGTHS: Free-spirited, very comfortable in her own fur, goes with the flow, enthusiastic

WEAKNESSES: Easily distracted, reckless driver, shares too much too early

PERSONAL HIGHLIGHT: Year living in the Scarribean making wind chimes out of scream shells

GOALS: Keeping the team smiling, becoming president of the Monsters, Inc., Party-Planning Committee

FAVORITE RECREATIONAL ACTIVITIES: Shokra yoga, competitive eating

EMERGENCY CONTACT: Double-T (BFF)

*Exceptionally chatty—initial interview took 28 hours—but has the kind of enthusiasm we want in an employee. Won the Rot Dog Eating Contest at the company picnic with 300 Rot Dogs . . . it was disturbing to watch, but we just couldn't look away.

Note to self:
Keep lunch away from her

VAL LITTLE

MIFT Driver Evaluation

NAME: Val Little

—Dangerously distracted in the rotunda

—Reckless racing on the Laugh Floor Access Hallway

—Terrifying turns in the tunnels

—Bold, balanced backups into service elevator, spooked Giant Eye in elevator

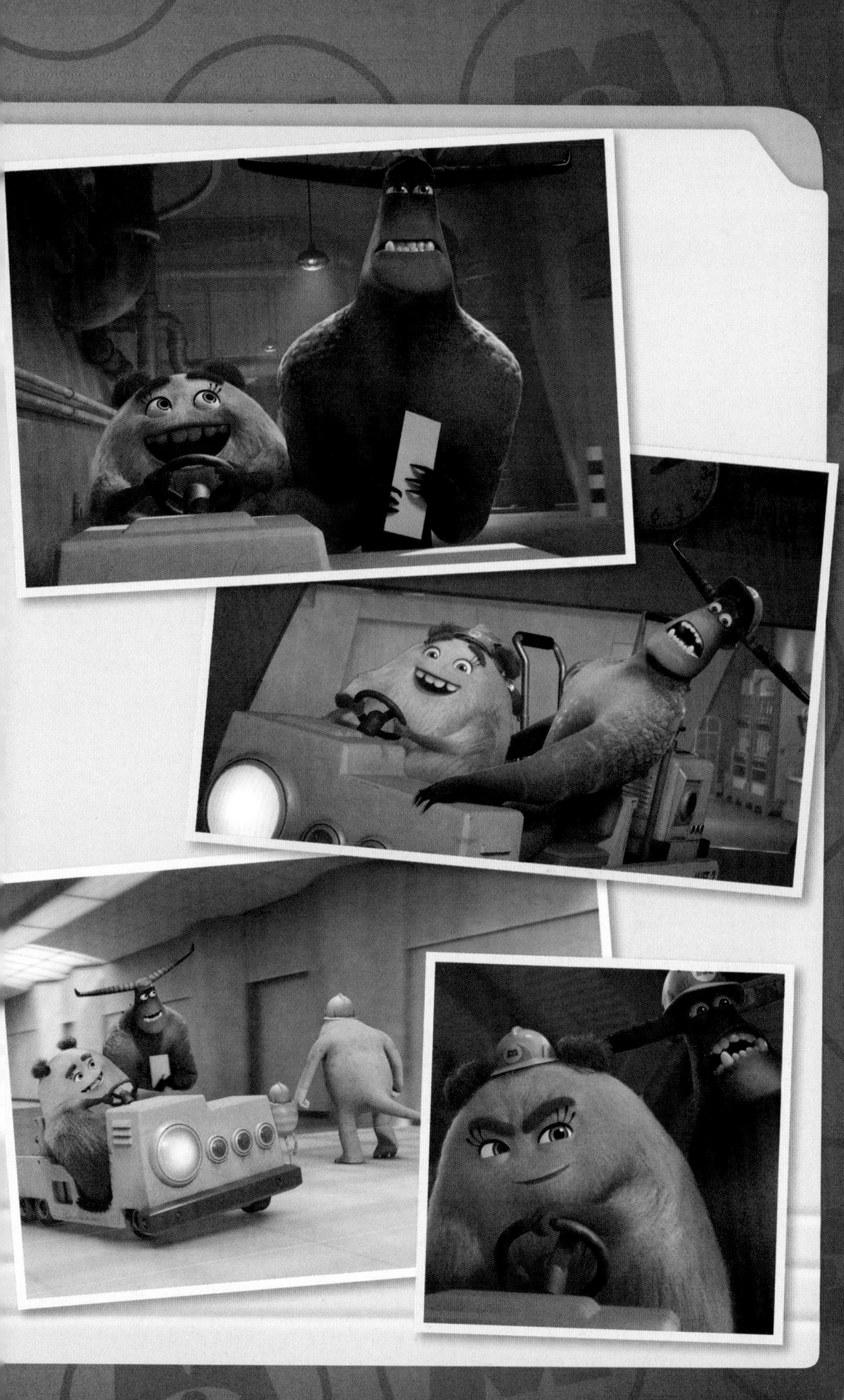

DUNCAN P. ANDERSON

STRENGTHS: Ambitious, organized, loving pet owner, coming up with new titles for himself on a weekly basis

WEAKNESSES: There are none —Duncan

PERSONAL HIGHLIGHT: Naming himself Deputy Supervisor of MIFT

GOALS: Taking Fritz's job

ADVANCED SKILLS: Delegating tasks to others, sucking up to authority figures, drafting semi-legal contracts, removing doohickeys, avoiding anything that involves muscular strength, eating an uncanny amount of Snotchos

EMERGENCY CONTACT: Roto, his emotional-support animal

**Eager to inform on fellow employees, but still shows that MIFT team spirit . . . as long as Fritz is watching, anyway*

IN
DUNCAN

IN
DUNCAN

DUNCAN P. ANDERSON

Dearest Diary,

An envious, moon-faced cretin by the name of Tylor Tuskmon butted his way into MIFT today. I'm not falling for his "Hey, I'm only here temporarily" lies—I can already smell the ambition on this . . . college boy. He wants Fritz's job. But I'm on to his little scheme!

Dear Diary,

You'll never guess what my cute little guy, Roto, did today. College Boy went to pet him and Roto nearly bit his finger off! He's such a precious little snookie-wookie-ookie-kins, I could just cuddle him all day long! Do you think he knows he's my best friend in the whole wide world? I hope he does. . . .

Dear Diary,

Had a LOT of trouble sleeping last night. Closed three of my eyes but the other one just kept peeking out. I can't remember if I told you—my tallest eye (I call him Topper) is more light-sensitive than the others—so it really enjoys darkness. And I get it, it's soothing, the thin stream of moonlight makes cool shadows on the wall. Who wouldn't want to stay up and enjoy that? Well, ME! That's who! I need some sleep! How will I ever become head of MIFT if I'm too tired to work!

KATHERINE STERNS

"CUTTER"

STRENGTHS: Rule follower, professional, tells it like it is

WEAKNESSES: Will work overtime, stubborn, scares other employees with her obsession with workplace-accident stories

PERSONAL HIGHLIGHT: Totally crushing karaoke at the Monsters, Inc., holiday party

GOALS: To memorize the latest version of the employee manual

MOST MEMORABLE WORKPLACE ACCIDENT: When Johnny went in to fix the pneumatic tube station and got himself sucked right up to the fifth floor. Well . . . his upper half, at least.

EMERGENCY CONTACT: Herself

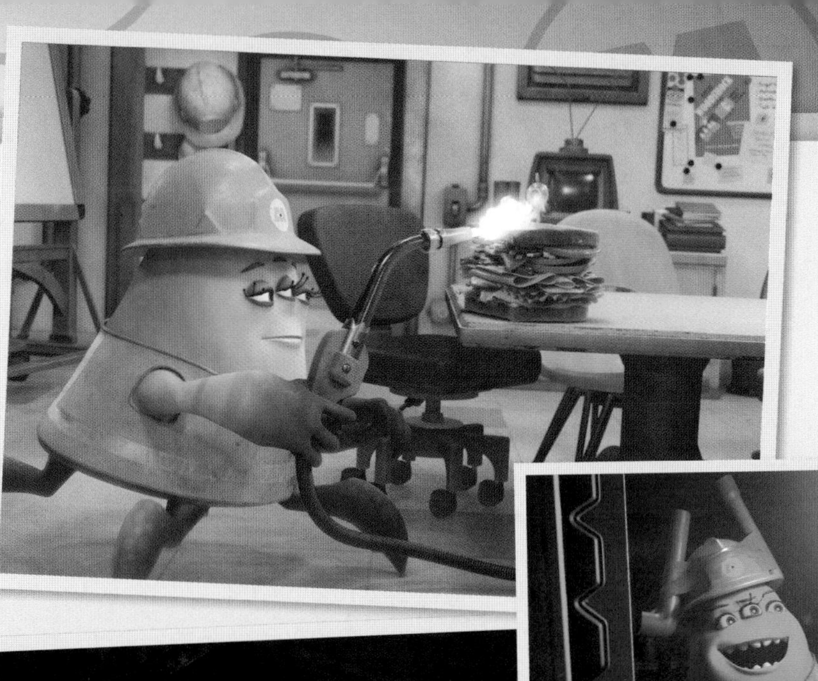

FOR REPAIRS

FRITZ

STRENGTHS: Fatherly, loyal, caring

WEAKNESSES: Believes too much in importance of MIFT, speeches can be long and a little boring, eccentric, has a hard time with common phrases

PERSONAL HIGHLIGHT: The "Boss of the Year" award the MIFT team gave him

GOALS: Proving the importance of the MIFT team to Monsters, Inc., leadership

ROLES HE'D LIKE TO HAVE: Father figure, grandfather figure, uncle-who's-divorced-from-Tylor's-biological-aunt-but-was-really-cool-so-he-just-keeps-in touch-and-sometimes-he-just-shows-up-out-of-the-blue figure

EMERGENCY CONTACT: MIFT family

Drooler Cooler

FRITZ

Fritz's
Motivational
MIFT Pitch
→

Since the day Monsters, Inc., was founded, there has been a need: a need for a dedicated team of mechanics to nurture the intricate machinery that is the very foundation of this factory. No matter how arduous or difficult the repair, MIFT is there to tighten the bolts, unclog the pipes, and wrench the nut. We embrace with unbridled participation what lies ahead!

And at the end of the day, we each say, "I am proud to be a member of the Monsters, Inc., Facilities Team."

FRITZ

WEEKLY PROD

	MONDAY	TUESDAY
9 AM	MIFT TEAM ROLL CALL	MIFT TEAM ROLL CALL
	NAP TIME	
10 AM	LAUGH FLOOR SAFETY MEETING	DOOR STATION REPAIR
11 AM	MAIL ROOM BREAK	MAIL ROOM BREAK
		PAY SMITTY AND NEEDLEMAN FOR ILLEGAL VACATION DOOR
12 PM	LAFFATERIA: MONSTER MASH MONDAY	LAFFATERIA: TERRIFYING TACO TUESDAY
1 PM	ENERGY CHECK	ENERGY CHECK
2 PM		LAUGH FLOOR ROUND 1 CUTS POSTED
	2ND NAP TIME	VENDING MACHINE RESTOCKING ask about new flavors of Drooler Cooler →
3 PM	LAUGH FLOOR AUDITIONS	KAIJU PREPAREDNESS DRILL
4 PM		LOBBY MAINTENANCE—EXIT SIDE DOOR
5 PM		

TION CALENDAR

ESDAY	THURSDAY	FRIDAY
ROLL CALL	MIFT TEAM ROLL CALL	MIFT TEAM ROLL CALL
D DAY! *—Make appointment to not get haircut*		*Don't forget to sign up!* VINTAGE DROOLER COOLER AUCTION SIGN-UP
FURBISHMENT *Val to buy more stickers*	LAUGH FLOOR SAFETY MEETING	EMPLOYEE ~~SCARE FAIR~~ *JEST FEST* IN THE ROTUNDA
OM BREAK	MAIL ROOM BREAK	MAIL ROOM BREAK
ATERIA: G WEDNESDAY	LAFFATERIA: $1 BARFALO WINGS D	
Y CHECK	ENERGY CHECK	
SCREAM IISTERS *Tylor's job*	SIMULATION ROOM CLEANINC	
	ALL DECOMMISSIONED DOORS DUE AT SHREDDER SHAFT	
DIVING AGAIN		**Ask Tylor what he means by "Stop showing up at my house after work, Fritz."*
	LAUGH FLOOR ROUND 2 CUTS POSTED	

ROTO

STRENGTHS: Loyal, agile, quick

WEAKNESSES: Aggressive, likes to bite, coughs hairballs

GOALS: Getting off the spinning wheel and out of the tank

HOME: Tank in the MIFT office

FAVORITE HIDING PLACE: Under the water cooler

TYLOR'S PET NAME: Little Vermin Ball

EMERGENCY CONTACT: Duncan

*BEWARE OF ROTO—he hisses, growls, and will bite.

ROTO

INCIDENCE REPORT

Description: Tylor left Roto's cage open, allowing him to escape.

10:14 AM

Tylor offers Roto a yummy treat.

10:15 AM

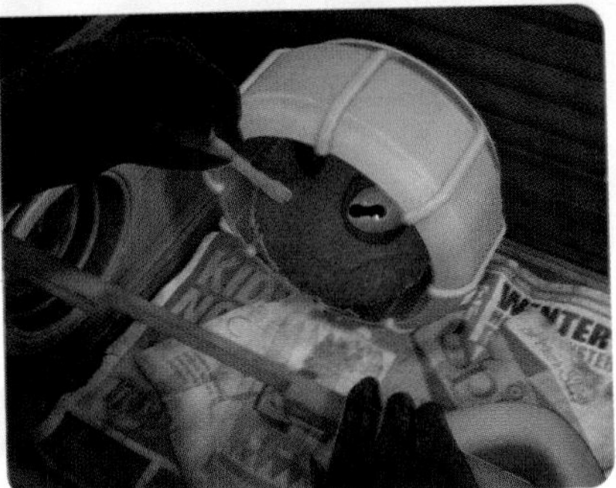

Roto declines. Tylor leaves the lid off Roto's cage.

10:16 AM

Roto escapes.

10:18 AM

Tylor continues to chase Roto around the MIFT office.

10:22 AM

Roto gets sucked into the tube transport.

10:28 AM

Tylor follows Roto through the tubes.

10:53 AM

Tylor returns Roto to his cage and firmly attaches the lid. The two agree to never speak of the incident again.

MONSTERS INC

WE RUN ON FUN!

SERVING GREATER MONSTROPOLIS

MONSTERS INC

bringing you the power of laughter

join our team today!

SERVING GREATER MONSTROPOLIS

THE MONSTERS, INC., EXECUTIVE TEAM

The Monsters, Inc., new leadership team is made up of pioneers in harnessing the power of laughter.

James P. Sullivan
Chief Executive Officer

Michael "Mike" Wazowski,
Senior Co-President of Monsters Inc., and Chief Executive Vice-Deputy Administrative Director of Comedy Resources Management (SC-POMIACEV-DADOCRM)

Roze
Key Master and Administrator

Celia Mae
Floor Supervisor

JAMES P. SULLIVAN

"SULLEY"

STRENGTHS: Tenacious, tough, devoted , former Top Scarer

WEAKNESSES: Keeping Mike in line, overly sentimental

PERSONAL HIGHLIGHT: Sneaking into a room and meeting his future best friend, Mike Wazowski, at Monsters University

GOALS: Increasing worker productivity and find Jokesters to fill the Laugh Floors

KEY STATS: Height: 7'8"
Weight: 766 lbs.
Birthday: August 17

EMERGENCY CONTACT: Bill Sullivan, father, famous Scarer

MICHAEL WAZOWSKI

"MIKE"

STRENGTHS: Funny, smart, fearless

WEAKNESSES: Impulsive, can be oblivious at times, reckless

PERSONAL HIGHLIGHT: Meeting his future best friend, Sulley, at Monsters University

GOALS: Teaching monsters to be funny

KEY STATS: Height: 3'9"
Weight: 148 lbs.
Birthday: November 16

EMERGENCY CONTACT: Celia Mae, girlfriend

HARRYHAUSEN'S
DINNER FOR 2,
SATURDAY AT 7 PM

DON'T BE LATE!

CELIA MAE

STRENGTHS: Efficient, organized, kind

WEAKNESSES: Suspicious

GOALS: Being promoted to Floor Manager

FAVORITE NICKNAMES FOR MIKE: Googley Bear, Googley Woogley

NAMES OF CELIA'S HAIR SNAKES: Ameila, Bobelia, Ophelia, Cordelia, Madge

EMERGENCY CONTACT: Michael Wazowski, boyfriend

MONSTERS, INC.

ROZE

STRENGTHS: Rule-follower, observant, actually enjoys paperwork, luscious pink hair

WEAKNESSES: Pungent odor, unsettling laughter, not as bubbly as her sister, receptive to Gary's charm

GOALS: To succeed where her sister failed and finally get Mike to file his paperwork on time

EMERGENCY CONTACT: Classified information

NEW HIRE

THE MONSTERS, INC., MAINTENANCE TEAM

Supportive co-workers of the monsters of the scare floor, Smitty and Needleman can sometimes get into trouble, but they always try their best.

Smitty

Needleman

INCIDENCE REPORT

Description: Incriminated themselves about having illegal vacation doors, slacked off work to play Sock Attack arcade game in Bowling Alley

—Fright Club members?
Need to follow up

MONSTERS INC.

We clown around to light our town

Serving Greater Monstropolis

JOIN OUR TEAM TODAY
MONSTERS INC
WE RUN ON FUN

AROUND THE OFFICE

We're Gearing Up
To Make You Smile
CLAWSON

Mr. Crummyham
Head of Monster Resources

Ms. Flint
Jokester Acquisition and Training Director

Currently working on employee reassignment and identifying monsters who may be effective Jokesters.

REASSIGNMENT

INCIDENCE REPORT

Description: The team has floundered a bit with their new assignment. They don't seem to be quite up to speed yet in making effective matches between employee ability and new roles on the Laugh Floor.

MEMO

TO: Mr. Crummyham

FROM: Ms. Flint

RE: Laugh Floor Training

Please keep this between us. I didn't want to share in our meeting with our new leaders, Sulley and Mike, but I'm terribly worried about our employees' ability to be funny. Scary—they're the tops. But I've been struggling to identify monsters who really have that natural comedic talent. We need to work on corporate culture—and add more professional development? Here are some ideas for workshops:

COMEDY COMMUNICATIONS: finding the words that get the best laughs

COMEDY PROP SELF-DEFENSE: protecting yourself against exploding whoopee cushions, runaway juggling balls, and rogue unicycles

MIRTHFUL MINDFULNESS: reducing stress and anxiety through the power of laughter

JOKE TIME MANAGEMENT: how to get to the punch line—FAST

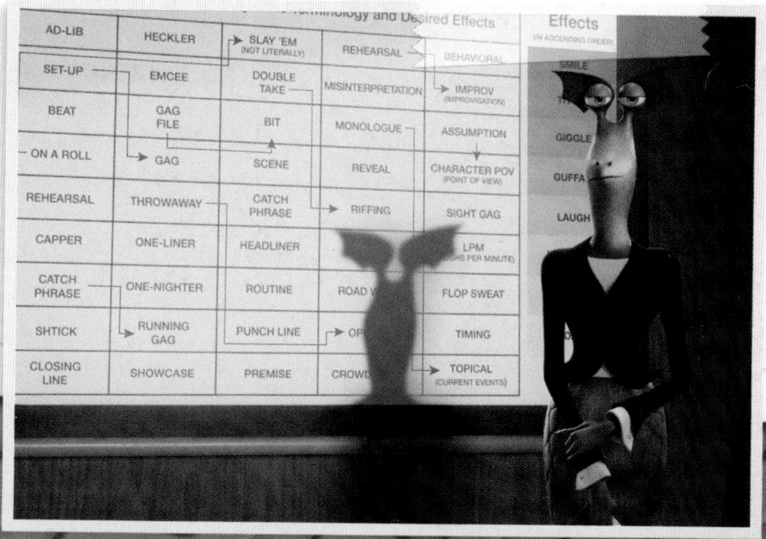

TODAY'S MENU

BREAKFAST BLITZ

ROTTEN EGGS BENEDICT

STENCH TOAST

FRESH MOLD CUP

COFFEE SCREAMER

LOSE YOUR LUNCH

CATERPILLAR CASSEROLE

MACARONI AND SLEAZE

SEWAGE SOUP

BARFALO WINGS — WARNING! Barfalo wings have been known to cause a stomach "thing"

ROAST BEAST

HAM AND SLEAZE

LAFFATERIA
MENU
Trampoline
Lessons
JOBS

KRISPY
SCREAMS
20%
OFF
COUPON

Drooler
Cooler
Classic
NEW!
BLORT

EMPLOYEE RECREATION FACILITY

GIBBERISH AS A SECOND LANGUAGE

CLASSES NOW FOAMING

Contact Monstropolis
Board Of Education

Classes Mon., Wed. and Fr

MONSTROPOLIS WREAKREATION CENTER

Space available for...
- *Meetings*
- *Conventions*
- *Exercise classes*
- *Night classes*

AND MORE!

All rental fees he
maintain our
infrastructure, roa
sidewalks, refuse a
snow removal.
Call 555-0101

Looking f
gloomma

2-bedroom tow
Private bo
$973 per month

555-0104

555-0100

555-0104

nce Lessons

555-0104

SCUMMAGE S

Annual Spring E

All proceeds to benefit the Greater Monstropolis United Charities

Taking d
no
Contrib
can be c
at t
Monstr
Comm
weekda

FUR CLUB FOR MONSTERS

A Furry Monster Is a Funny Monster

Revolutionary formula sprouts fur in the desert that was once your head!

Call now for your risk free trial of ROFURGROW!
1-800-555-0199

ADVANCED CLAW & FUR CARE

- APPOINTMENTS ONLY -
Call the Claw Doctor at
555-CLIPS-R-US

JOIN TEA FUNNY STU

Study with your monster friends and Comed

- Friday nights from 7-10 p.m. -

ed to learn some new jokes? Struggling with your pranks? You're not alone!

Join our study group—we've asked some of Monstropolis's greatest comedy minds to join us by videoconference—(still waiting for a response). And en if you don't get your comedy act together, you'll e able to share your feelings with other monsters who are struggling to be funny just like you!

- *Agooities*
- *Fleatirement Planning*
- *Living On Fixed Grimcome*
- *Anti-social Security*

Free! Every other Tuesday at the Monstropolis Wreck Center

WELCOME TO THE LAUGH FLOOR!

Joining the Laugh Floor team?
Helping Monsters, Inc., transition to our new mission?
It's important to keep these rules in mind.

MIKE'S 10 RULES OF COMEDY

1. Punch line does not mean punching someone.
2. Don't howl at your own jokes.
3. Tentacles: funny
   Razor-sharp claws: not funny
4. Multiple heads should speak one at a time.
5. No claws for tickling.
6. Scared kids don't laugh.
7. Don't hurt the audience.
8. Always keep sharp spikes in!
9. You won't get a laugh if you don't take a bath.
10. Never let them see you slobber.

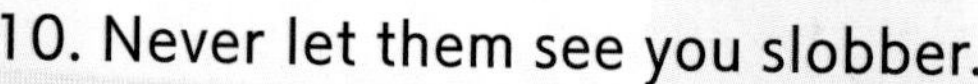

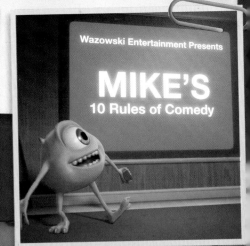

THE DANGERS OF COMEDY

A message from the desk of Michael Wazowski

To: All Monsters, Inc., Monsters

Listen, I read Sulley's letter—and I know he was trying to sound all formal and like a Waternoose-level CEO and everything, without the criminal element, of course, but it's real simple.

We need to get these kids to laugh! I'm telling you—TEN TIMES the power of screams!

It's the best way to save our company—and our jobs.

I know for some of you, that's a big challenge—you're not comedically gifted like yours truly. But give it a try. I'm always here to help.

The doors to my Comedy Class are always open (metaphorically, of course; after some noise complaints, we had to start keeping the door closed at all times).

And I promise, we can do this if we do it together.

Your pal,

MIKE

Senior Co-President of Monsters, Inc., and Chief Executive Vice-Deputy Administrative Director of Comedy Resources Management (SC-POMIACEV-DADOCRM)